PRISTINE POEMS INDIA

M V TRYST

ISBN 978-93-5667-618-3
© M V TRYST 2023

Published in India 2023 by Pencil

A brand of
One Point Six Technologies Pvt. Ltd.
Unit no. 26, Ground Floor, Building A1,
Wadala Truck Terminal Road,
Near Post Office, Antop Hill, Mumbai - 400037
E connect@thepencilapp.com
W www.thepencilapp.com

Author biography

M V Tryst is the poet of 'Pristine Poems'.
Tryst had a good experience in writing and is an eloquent speaker and writer.
Tryst is a student in Finance and Economics.

Tryst is a polyglot and is interested in learning history and cultures across the world.
Tryst loves to learn and share knowledge, and facts about the world through various sources in fictional, non-fictional, and poetic ways.

'Pristine Poems' is a series of poems about a place. This book is about India.

CONTENTS

INDIA

India, a land of mystique and wonder,

A place where ancient meets modern thunder,

From the snow-capped peaks of the Himalayas,

To the golden sands of the southern bays.

In the bustling streets of Mumbai,

To the serene temples of Rishikesh high,

The colors, the sounds, the smells,

A sensory feast, the heart swells.

The Taj Mahal, a true masterpiece,

An ode to love, a symbol of peace,

The forts and palaces, a regal sight,

A testament to India's glorious might.

The Ganges, a sacred river divine,

A pilgrimage site for the faithful's shrine,

The yoga and meditation, a spiritual quest,

A quest for the soul, a lifelong quest.

The spices, the flavors, the taste,
A cuisine that's eclectic and great,
From the tangy chaats to the sweet jalebis,
The food is a treat, an absolute bliss.

India, a land of diversity,
A place where cultures meet in harmony,
From the festivals of Holi to Diwali,
India's vibrancy is an endless rally.

A nation of a billion hearts,
A place where unity never departs,
India, the land of my birth,
A place that forever holds my worth.

India, the land of the rising sun,
Where every day is a new battle won,
The land of the brave, the land of the free,
A place where everyone can truly be.

From the green fields of Punjab,
To the blue waters of Kerala,
India's beauty is beyond compare,
Its diversity unmatched anywhere.

PRISTINE POEMS INDIA

The sounds of the sitar and tabla,
Echo through the streets and hills,
The music and dance of India,
Is a joy that forever fills.

The sun-kissed deserts of Rajasthan,
The lush green forests of Assam,
India's landscapes are so vast,
Its beauty will forever last.

The warmth of the people, their hospitality,
Is a reflection of their kindness and morality,
From the rickshaw pullers to the CEOs,
India's progress and potential grows.

India, a country so full of life,
A place where traditions meet with strife,
A place where cultures and religions unite,
India, a land of endless delight.

So here's to India, a land so grand,
A place that will forever stand,
With its diverse cultures and ancient past,
India's future is bright and steadfast.

India, a land of contrasts and contradictions,
Where the old and new coexist with no restrictions,
The hustle and bustle of city life,
Is balanced by the calmness of village life.

The monuments and ruins of centuries gone by,
Stand tall, telling stories that never die,
The pride of India, its glorious past,
Is a reminder that its heritage will forever last.

The languages, the dialects, the accents so diverse,
Reflect the nation's unity, its strength and its verse,
From Hindi to Bengali, from Tamil to Punjabi,
India's languages are a celebration of its diversity.

The wildlife, the forests, the mountains and the seas,
Are home to a rich biodiversity,
From tigers to elephants, from peacocks to snakes,
India's fauna is a treasure for all to embrace.

The women of India, so strong and resilient,
Are the backbone of its progress and development,
From science to sports, from arts to entrepreneurship,
India's women are breaking barriers with no impediments.

India, a country that has come so far,
Yet has so much potential to reach for the stars,
With its people, its culture, and its might,
India's future is a shining light.

India, a land of innovation and creativity,
Where new ideas are born with great intensity,
From the IT hubs of Bangalore and Hyderabad,
To the startups of Mumbai and Ahmedabad.

The education system, with its focus on knowledge,
Has produced leaders and thinkers that the world will acknowledge,
From Tagore to Gandhi, from Bose to Nehru,
India's thinkers have left an impact that's true.

The spirituality and philosophy of ancient India,
Has had a profound impact across the world's diaspora,
From yoga to meditation, from Ayurveda to Vedic knowledge,
India's wisdom has helped humanity seek solace.

The food of India, a fusion of flavors and spices,
Is a delight for the senses, a treat that entices,
From the biryanis of Hyderabad to the dosas of Chennai,
India's cuisine is a culinary journey that never ends.

PRISTINE POEMS INDIA

India, a land of contrasts and beauty,
A place where ancient meets modernity,
A nation with so much to offer and give,
India, a land where the heart can forever live.

India, the land of colors and hues,
A place where beauty is never a ruse,
From the majestic mountains to the rolling plains,
India's beauty is a sight that forever remains.

India, a land of diverse cultures,
Is a tapestry of beauty that forever endures,
From the regal palaces of Rajasthan,
To the serene backwaters of Kerala's plan.

India, a place of infinite beauty,
Where nature and history meet with great bounty,
From the iconic Taj Mahal to the Red Fort,
India's architecture is a marvel that can't be fought.

India's beauty lies in its people,
Whose warmth and hospitality are truly ample,
From the bustling streets of Delhi to the quiet villages of Goa,
India's people make the beauty glow.

India, a land of art and craft,
Is a canvas where creativity is never daft,
From the intricate textiles of Gujarat,
To the dazzling jewelry of the Rajasthani hat.

India, a land of music and dance,
Is a rhythm that forever enchants,
From the classical beats of Bharatanatyam,
To the lively tunes of Bhangra's charm.

India's beauty is in its festivals,
Where cultures and traditions meet with no hurdles,
From the colorful Holi to the festive Diwali,
India's festivals are a sight that's truly jolly.

India, a land of spirituality,
Is a beauty that goes beyond all rationality,
From the holy Ganges to the peaceful ashrams,
India's spirituality is a beauty that forever calms.

India, a land of natural wonders,
Is a beauty that fills hearts with thunder,
From the snow-capped peaks of the Himalayas,
To the pristine beaches of Andaman's bays.

India's beauty is in its history,
Where the past and present meet with mystery,
From the ancient caves of Ajanta and Ellora,
To the historic ruins of Hampi and Gwalior.

India's beauty is in its cuisine,
Where flavors and spices are a colorful sheen,
From the rich curries of North India,
To the tangy chutneys of South India.

India's beauty is in its sports,
Where passion and skill are never shorts,
From the cricket grounds of Mumbai and Kolkata,
To the hockey fields of Bangalore and New Delhi.

India's beauty is in its diversity,
Where differences are a bond that's free,
From the unity of its people to its varied landscapes,
India's beauty is a treasure that's never at an escape.

India's beauty is in its language,
Where words and expressions are a cultural baggage,
From the poetic Urdu to the melodious Kannada,
India's languages are a beauty that forever binds ya.

India's beauty is in its democracy,
Where the power of the people is a shining reciprocity,
From the peaceful protests of its citizens,
To the free and fair elections of its republic's missions.

India, a land of spices and flavors,
Where food is a celebration that never wavers,
From the savory curries to the sweet desserts,
Indian food is a culinary journey that never hurts.

The aromas of cumin, coriander, and cardamom,
Fill the air with a fragrance that's seldom calm,
From the buttery naans to the crispy dosas,
Indian food is a journey that never pauses.

The rich gravies of paneer and chicken,
Are a treat for the senses, a delight that's never thin,
From the tangy chutneys to the creamy raitas,
Indian food is a journey that never falters.

The biryanis, the kebabs, the tandooris,
Are a feast for the taste buds, a journey that's truly glorious,
From the spicy vindaloos to the mild kormas,
Indian food is a journey that forever transforms.

The sweets, the desserts, the confectionaries,
Are a delight for the soul, a treat that's never contrary,
From the mouth-watering gulab jamuns to the creamy kulfi,
Indian food is a journey that's truly leafy.

The tea, the coffee, the lassis and chaas,
Are a refreshing sip, a thirst that forever surpass,
From the spiced chai to the refreshing nimbu paani,
Indian food is a journey that forever sunny.

India, a land of food that's diverse,
Is a canvas where flavors and spices converge,
From the north to the south, from the east to the west,
Indian food is a journey that's forever at its best.

In the bustling streets and crowded bazaars,
Food is a feast for the senses, a treat that never jars,
From the samosas to the vadas and pakoras,
Indian food is a journey that's never boring or blasé.

The thalis, the platters, the lunch and dinner plates,
Are a riot of colors, a meal that never waits,
From the dal makhani to the palak paneer,
Indian food is a journey that's always so dear.

The street food, the chaat, the pani puri,
Are a snack that's so tempting, a taste that's truly fury,
From the spicy tikkas to the savory dabeli,
Indian food is a journey that's forever so bubbly.

The pickles, the chutneys, the sauces and dips,
Are a condiment that's so flavorful, a taste that never skips,
From the tangy tomato chutney to the sweet mango pickle,
Indian food is a journey that's forever so fickle.

India, a land of food that's so vibrant,
Is a feast for the senses, a cuisine that's so jubilant,
From the rich Mughlai to the subtle Jain,
Indian food is a journey that's forever so gain.

So come, take a bite, and savor the flavors,
India's food is a journey that never waivers,
From the rich masalas to the subtle spices,
Indian food is a journey that's forever so priceless.

India, a land of art that's so diverse,
Is a canvas where creativity never submerges,
From the intricate sculptures to the vibrant paintings,
Indian art is a journey that's truly entertaining.

The majestic temples and their carvings,
Are a wonder of architecture, a sight that's never starving,
From the intricate reliefs to the towering gopurams,
Indian art is a journey that forever stuns.

The classical dances and their movements,
Are a feast for the eyes, a spectacle that's never dormant,
From the grace of Bharatanatyam to the energy of Bhangra,
Indian art is a journey that forever inspires.

The music and its melodies,
Are a treat for the ears, a symphony that's never belies,
From the classical ragas to the popular film songs,
Indian art is a journey that forever throngs.

The handicrafts, the textiles, and their embroidery,
Are a marvel of skill, a craft that's never ordinary,
From the intricate zardozi to the colorful bandhani,
Indian art is a journey that forever enchants.

The folk art and their motifs,
Are a celebration of culture, a tradition that forever uplifts,
From the Warli paintings to the Madhubani art,
Indian art is a journey that's forever a part.

India, a land of art that's so rich,

Is a journey that forever never switch,

From the ancient to the contemporary,

Indian art is a journey that's forever legendary.

The poetry and literature and their nuances,

Are a celebration of language, a heritage that forever advances,

From the epics of Ramayana and Mahabharata,

Indian art is a journey that forever never detracts.

The cinema and its storytelling,

Are a reflection of society, a narrative that's forever compelling,

From the classics of Satyajit Ray to the blockbusters of Bollywood,

Indian art is a journey that forever enfold.

The calligraphy and typography and their beauty,

Are a mastery of writing, an art that's forever so groovy,

From the Devanagari script to the Urdu Nastaliq,

Indian art is a journey that forever never flick.

The street art and graffiti and their expression,

Are a voice of rebellion, a message that's forever in session,

From the murals of Mumbai to the wall art of Delhi,

Indian art is a journey that's forever so belly.

The photography and its moments,

Are a capture of life, a vision that's forever so potent,

From the works of Raghu Rai to the snapshots of Steve McCurry,

Indian art is a journey that forever never flurry.

India, a land of art that's so profound,

Is a kaleidoscope where colors and textures abound,

From the traditional to the contemporary,

Indian art is a journey that's forever so radiant and necessary.

India, a land of history so vast,

Is a treasure trove where stories forever last,

From the ancient civilization of the Indus Valley,

Indian history is a journey that's truly holy.

The tales of the mighty empires and their reigns,

Are a chronicle of power, a saga that forever remains,

From the Mauryas to the Mughals,

Indian history is a journey that's forever so magical.

The struggles for independence and their heroes,

Are a tribute to courage, a legacy that forever glows,

From the non-violent movements of Gandhi to the militant revolt of
Bhagat Singh,

Indian history is a journey that forever rings.

The diversity of culture and its evolution,
Are a showcase of heritage, a legacy that forever prevails,
From the Sanskrit literature to the regional languages,
Indian history is a journey that forever never cages.

The discoveries and inventions and their impact,
Are a testament to knowledge, a contribution that forever stacks,
From the ancient science of Ayurveda to the modern space program,
Indian history is a journey that forever never slum.

India, a land of history so rich,
Is a narrative that's forever never switch,
From the past to the present,
Indian history is a journey that's forever relevant.

So come, take a step, and travel through time,
India's history is a journey that forever never mime,
From the ancient to the modern,
Indian history is a journey that's forever so sovereign.

India, a land of great personalities so many,
Is a treasure trove where inspiration forever plenty,
From the leaders of the freedom struggle to the modern-day heroes,
Indian personalities are a journey that forever glows.

The father of the nation, Mahatma Gandhi,
Is a symbol of peace, a leader who forever rally,
His non-violent resistance and his message of love,
Is an inspiration that forever never shove.

The first prime minister, Jawaharlal Nehru,
Is a visionary, a statesman who forever drew,
His modernizing policies and his love for democracy,
Is a legacy that forever never seize.

The queen of melody, Lata Mangeshkar,
Is a voice of magic, a singer who forever never blur,
Her timeless songs and her contribution to music,
Is a journey that forever never lose its tick.

The master of poetry, Rabindranath Tagore,
Is a genius, a writer who forever never bore,
His immortal works and his message of humanity,
Is a treasure that forever never vanity.

The cricketing legend, Sachin Tendulkar,
Is a maestro, a sportsman who forever forever never submerges,
His records and his passion for the game,
Is a legacy that forever never tame.

The former president, Dr. A.P.J. Abdul Kalam,
Is a scientist, a teacher who forever forever never calm,
His contribution to space and his message of education,
Is an inspiration that forever never bow to any situation.

India, a land of great personalities so many,
Is a journey that forever never just any,
From the ancient to the modern,
Indian personalities are a treasure that forever never weakened.

The queen of dance, Padma Subrahmanyam,
Is a performer, a guru who forever never condemn,
Her classical art and her devotion to Bharatanatyam,
Is a legacy that forever never stem.

The social reformer, Raja Ram Mohan Roy,
Is a pioneer, an activist who forever never coy,
His campaign for women's rights and his fight against Sati,
Is a journey that forever never go tiptoe.

The poet of the masses, Harivansh Rai Bachchan,
Is a wordsmith, a lyricist who forever never flinch,
His immortal works and his message of hope,
Is an inspiration that forever never mope.

The legendary filmmaker, Satyajit Ray,
Is a storyteller, a director who forever never sway,
His classic films and his contribution to world cinema,
Is a journey that forever never insignia.

The social worker, Mother Teresa,
Is an angel, a humanitarian who forever never hysteria,
Her selfless service and her message of love,
Is a legacy that forever never shove.

The badminton sensation, Saina Nehwal,
Is a champion, a player who forever never fall,
Her triumphs and her dedication to the game,
Is an inspiration that forever never tame.

India, a land of great personalities so many,
Is a journey that forever never less than any,
From the past to the present,
Indian personalities are a treasure that forever never absent.

India, a land of achievements so many,
Is a treasure trove where discoveries forever plenty,
From the ancient science of Ayurveda to the modern-day space missions,
Indian achievements are a journey that forever never inhibition.

The invention of the decimal system,
Is a contribution, a legacy that forever never random,
From the ancient mathematicians to the modern-day scientists,
Indian discoveries are a journey that forever never pessimists.

The ancient science of Ayurveda and Yoga,
Are practices of health, a way of life that forever never boga,
From the sages of the past to the modern-day gurus,
Indian achievements are a journey that forever never obscure.

The discovery of the zero and the concept of infinity,
Are concepts of mathematics, a legacy that forever never finity,
From the ancient scholars to the modern-day mathematicians,
Indian discoveries are a journey that forever never assumptions.

The launch of the first satellite, Aryabhata,
Is a milestone, an achievement that forever never mata,
From the scientists of the past to the modern-day space explorers,
Indian achievements are a journey that forever never abhors.

The development of the world's smallest satellite, KalamSat,
Is a breakthrough, a triumph that forever never batt,
From the students of the past to the modern-day innovators,
Indian achievements are a journey that forever never gators.

India, a land of achievements so many,

Is a journey that forever never any,

From the past to the present,

Indian achievements are a treasure that forever never absent.

The quest for a healthy nation,

Is a mission, a dream that forever never regression,

From the present to the future,

Health is a journey that forever requires culture.

India, a land of ancient history and vibrant culture,

Is a nation that forever never fails to allure,

From the Himalayan peaks to the sandy shores,

India's greatness is a journey that forever never bores.

The land of rich art and literature,

Is a canvas, a masterpiece that forever never feature,

From the epics of Ramayana and Mahabharata,

India's greatness is a journey that forever never nata.

The home of world-renowned cuisine and spices,

Is a flavor, a taste that forever never misses,

From the North to the South,

India's greatness is a journey that forever never drouth.

The land of great leaders and freedom fighters,
Is a legacy, a tribute that forever never lighters,
From Gandhi to Nehru,
India's greatness is a journey that forever never bleu.

The hub of modern technology and innovation,
Is a progress, a development that forever never ration,
From space missions to software,
India's greatness is a journey that forever never core.

India, a land of ancient history and vibrant culture,
Is a nation that forever never fails to allure,
From the past to the present,
India's greatness is a journey that forever never absent.

India, a land of diverse cultures and heritage,
Is a nation that forever never loses its courage,
From the mighty Himalayas to the golden sand,
India's beauty is a journey that forever never bland.

The birthplace of great sages and saints,
Is a destination, a pilgrimage that forever never faints,
From the holy river Ganges to the ancient temples,
India's spirituality is a journey that forever never simple.

The home of ancient art and architecture,

Is a treasure, a masterpiece that forever never rupture,

From the magnificent Taj Mahal to the great forts,

India's beauty is a journey that forever never shorts.

The land of vibrant festivals and celebrations,

Is a culture, a tradition that forever never hesitations,

From Diwali to Holi,

India's joy is a journey that forever never lowly.

The birthplace of great leaders and thinkers,

Is a legacy, a tribute that forever never blinks,

From Mahatma Gandhi to Rabindranath Tagore,

India's wisdom is a journey that forever never bore.

The hub of modern innovation and development,

Is a progress, a growth that forever never resent,

From the IT industry to space missions,

India's achievements are a journey that forever never omissions.

India, a land of diverse cultures and heritage,

Is a nation that forever never loses its courage,

From the past to the present,

India's greatness is a journey that forever never absent.

India, a land of natural beauty,
Is a sight that forever never duty,
From the lush green forests to the pristine beaches,
India's nature is a journey that forever never ceases.

The majestic mountains of the Himalayas,
Is a wonder, a sight that forever never betrays,
From the snow-capped peaks to the serene valleys,
India's nature is a journey that forever never rallies.

The vast plains of the Deccan plateau,
Is a landscape, a horizon that forever never low,
From the rolling hills to the vast grasslands,
India's nature is a journey that forever never strands.

The dense tropical forests of the Western Ghats,
Is a treasure, a paradise that forever never chats,
From the exotic flora to the endangered fauna,
India's nature is a journey that forever never drama.

The pristine beaches of the Andaman and Nicobar,
Is a paradise, a serenity that forever never jar,
From the turquoise waters to the white sands,
India's nature is a journey that forever never disbands.

India, a land of natural beauty,
Is a sight that forever never duty,
From the past to the future,
India's nature is a journey that forever never nurture.

India, a land of culture and tradition,
Is a nation that deserves our utmost admiration,
From the ancient scriptures to the modern times,
India's legacy is a journey that forever never declines.

The diversity of languages, religions, and customs,
Is a harmony, a unity that forever never rumbles,
From the northern Himalayas to the southern coast,
India's culture is a journey that forever never boasts.

The rich heritage of art, music, and literature,
Is a creativity, an expression that forever never falters,
From the classical dances to the modern cinema,
India's art is a journey that forever never tremors.

India, the land of diversity,
A country of immense geography.
From the mighty Himalayas in the north,
To the vast Indian Ocean in the south.

The Himalayas, the world's highest mountain range,
Proudly standing as India's crown and change.
With snow-capped peaks and deep valleys,
Home to diverse flora and fauna.

The northern plains, a vast alluvial land,
Fertile and flat, nurtured by the Ganges' hand.
With numerous rivers flowing through,
Life thrives in this lush region too.

The Deccan plateau, in the heart of India,
A land of rocks, plateaus, and savannah.
With rich mineral resources and ancient heritage,
It's a land of legends and stories to cherish.

The Western Ghats, a long mountain range,
Stretching parallel to India's western coast range.
A biodiversity hotspot with lush forests and wildlife,
A treasure trove of natural beauty and cultural delight.

The Eastern Ghats, a chain of hills and valleys,
Running along India's eastern border with ease.
With diverse landscapes and rich cultural heritage,
It's a land of ancient wisdom and timeless treasure.

The coastal plains, surrounded by seas,
A hub of trade and commerce, bustling with ease.
With sandy beaches, backwaters, and mangrove forests,
It's a land of beauty and bounty, always at its best.

The Andaman and Nicobar Islands, a cluster of jewels,
A paradise on earth, with crystal clear waters and sandy pools.

With pristine beaches and vibrant marine life,
It's a world of its own, a true paradise.

India, a land of diverse geography,
A treasure trove of natural beauty and cultural legacy.
With its mountains, plains, and coasts,
It's a land of wonders, waiting to be explored and boast.

India, the land of kings and queens,
A land of stories, legends, and dreams.
From the mighty emperors of the past,
To the valiant warriors that stood fast.

King Ashoka, the great Mauryan king,
A ruthless conqueror turned a man of peace within.
He embraced Buddhism and preached non-violence,
A legacy that still resonates in Indian conscience.

King Harsha, the great emperor of Kannauj,
A patron of art, culture, and learning too.
He hosted grand assemblies and festivals,
A time of prosperity and cultural revival.

King Krishnadevaraya, the Vijayanagara king,
A warrior, scholar, and patron of arts in everything.
His reign was a golden age of literature and music,
A time of grandeur, grace, and artistic magic.

King Akbar, the Mughal emperor supreme,
A visionary ruler with a grand dream.
He expanded his empire and embraced diversity,

A legacy of tolerance, harmony, and unity.

King Shivaji, the Maratha warrior king,
A valiant fighter and defender of his land and kin.
He fought against the mighty Mughal empire,
A symbol of courage, valor, and pride.

King Tipu Sultan, the tiger of Mysore,
A brave and visionary ruler, forever more.
He fought against the British with all his might,
A hero of resistance, freedom, and rights.

King Raja Raja Chola, the great Tamil king,
A patron of art, architecture, and everything.
He built the grand Brihadeeswara temple,
A masterpiece of ancient engineering and temple.

King Prithviraj Chauhan, the Rajput king,
A legendary warrior with a noble ring.
He fought against the mighty Muhammad Ghori,
A symbol of valor, honor, and glory.

King Chandragupta Maurya, the first Mauryan king,
A visionary ruler who established a mighty thing.
He unified India and laid the foundation,
A legacy of strength, power, and expansion.

King Vikramaditya, the legendary king,
A patron of learning and wisdom, everything.
He hosted the grand Vikram Samvat era,
A time of knowledge, culture, and gala.

India, a land of kings and queens,
A land of stories, legends, and dreams.
From the ancient past to the modern age,
Their legacies still inspire and engage.

Kohinoor, the diamond of legend and fame,
A priceless jewel with a storied name.
From the mines of Golconda it came,
A symbol of power, wealth, and acclaim.

From the hands of Rajas and Sultans it passed,
A trophy of conquest, a prize of the past.
Its journey was long, its story vast,
A tale of intrigue, power, and contrast.

It was worn by kings and queens of yore,
A symbol of their might, glory, and more.
It adorned crowns and scepters galore,
A treasure of royalty, forever more.

But its beauty and shine attracted eyes,
Of foreign invaders, with deceitful lies.
They coveted it, their greed never dies,
They took it away, with cunning and guise.

It changed hands, from East to West,
From India to Persia, to Britain, and the rest.
It was cut and polished, its size reduced,
Its worth diminished, but still, it amused.

Today it sits, in a British crown,
A reminder of its history and renown.
It's a symbol of conquest, greed, and renown,
A part of India's legacy, forever known.

Kohinoor, the diamond of legend and fame,
A priceless jewel with a storied name.
Its journey was long, its story vast,
A tale of intrigue, power, and contrast.

India, the land of rivers divine,
A network of lifelines that intertwine.
From the Himalayan snows to the sea,
They flow with might, power, and majesty.

The Ganges, the holy river supreme,
A symbol of India's spiritual dream.
It flows through plains, hills, and streams,
A source of life, purity, and esteem.

It's a river of faith, worship, and devotion,
A pilgrimage site for the faithful in motion.
From the Ghats of Varanasi to the delta's end,
It's a river of hope, love, and transcend.

The Yamuna, the sister river of Ganga,
A tributary that flows with zeal and vigour.
It's a river of history, culture, and valor,
A witness to India's past, present, and future.

It's a river of love, devotion, and charm,

A symbol of Radha-Krishna's divine farm.
From the Taj Mahal to the Kumbh Mela,
It's a river of hope, faith, and gala.

The Brahmaputra, the river of the East,
A mighty river that never rests.
It flows through Assam's lush forests and hills,
A source of life, commerce, and thrill.

It's a river of nature, wildlife, and culture,
A land of tea, silk, and agriculture.
From the Kaziranga to the Kamakhya,
It's a river of beauty, mystery, and ahimsa.

The Godavari, the river of the South,
A river that flows with a spiritual mouth.
It's a river of literature, music, and art,
A source of inspiration, culture, and heart.

It's a river of pilgrims, festivals, and faith,
A land of legends, stories, and grace.
From the Nashik Kumbh to the Bhadrachalam,
It's a river of joy, bliss, and calm.

The Narmada, the river of the West,
A river of love, devotion, and zest.
It flows through mountains, hills, and plains,
A source of life, hope, and gains.

It's a river of spirituality, nature, and charm,
A symbol of the goddess, her love, and her harm.
From the Omkareshwar to the Maheshwar,

It's a river of faith, culture, and bower.

The Kaveri, the river of the South,
A river that flows with a cultural mouth.
It's a river of agriculture, music, and dance,
A source of joy, prosperity, and chance.

It's a river of devotion, worship, and grace,
A land of temples, festivals, and space.
From the Srirangam to the Kaveri delta,
It's a river of tradition, history, and delta.

India, a land of rivers divine,
A network of lifelines that intertwine.
From the mighty Himalayas to the sea,
They flow with might, power, and majesty.

They are a source of life, hope, and gain,
A symbol of India's spiritual terrain.
They are a part of India's cultural bower,
A land of rivers divine, forever more.

India, the land of dance and rhythm,
A land of diversity, culture, and hymn.
From classical to folk, they all chime in,
A celebration of life, love, and sin.

Bharatanatyam, the dance of Tamil Nadu,
A classical dance that's deep and true.
It's a dance of grace, beauty, and cue,
A dance of devotion, love, and virtue.

It's a dance of stories, myths, and legends,
A dance of abhinaya, mudras, and bends.
From the temples of Chidambaram to Madurai,
It's a dance of history, culture, and fly.

Kathak, the dance of the North,
A classical dance that's rich and forth.
It's a dance of storytelling, music, and girth,
A dance of grace, beauty, and worth.

It's a dance of the Mughals, their style and flair,
A dance of fusion, culture, and care.
From the ghats of Varanasi to the court of Akbar,
It's a dance of history, tradition, and scar.

Kuchipudi, the dance of Andhra Pradesh,
A classical dance that's rooted and blessed.
It's a dance of devotion, love, and zest,
A dance of grace, beauty, and fest.

It's a dance of the temples, their tales and lore,
A dance of abhinaya, nritta, and more.
From the Krishna temple of Srikakulam to the Golkonda Fort,
It's a dance of history, culture, and port.

Odissi, the dance of Orissa,
A classical dance that's divine and bliss.
It's a dance of grace, beauty, and hiss,
A dance of devotion, love, and hiss.

It's a dance of the temples, their art and grace,
A dance of abhinaya, mudras, and pace.
From the Konark Sun Temple to the Jagannath Puri,
It's a dance of history, culture, and jury.

Mohiniyattam, the dance of Kerala,
A classical dance that's subtle and mella.
It's a dance of grace, beauty, and drella,
A dance of devotion, love, and bella.

It's a dance of the temples, their art and soul,
A dance of abhinaya, mudras, and roll.
From the Koothambalam to the backwaters of Alleppey,
It's a dance of history, culture, and sway.

Manipuri, the dance of Manipur,
A classical dance that's pure and sure.
It's a dance of grace, beauty, and lure,
A dance of devotion, love, and cure.

It's a dance of the temples, their gods and lore,
A dance of abhinaya, mudras, and more.
From the Ras Lila of Manipur to the Imphal valley,
It's a dance of history, culture, and rally.

Dandiya, the dance of Gujarat,
A folk dance that's fun and fat.
It's a dance of joy, music, and that,
A dance of love, celebration, and hat.

It's a dance of the Navratri, the nine nights of fun,
A dance of circles, sticks, and pun.

From the Rann of Kutch to the Sabarmati river,
It's a dance of culture, tradition, and liver.

Bhangra, the dance of Punjab,
A folk dance that's bold and grand.
It's a dance of joy, music, and band,
A dance of love, celebration, and land.

India, the land of diversity,
A country of many states, each with its own identity.
From the Himalayas in the north,
To the oceans in the south, east, and west, henceforth.

Kashmir, the paradise on earth,
A state with a beauty beyond any worth.
From the snow-capped mountains to the Dal Lake,
It's a land of enchantment, beauty, and make.

Himachal Pradesh, the land of snow,
A state with a charm that's hard to let go.
From the valleys of Manali to the peaks of Rohtang Pass,
It's a land of adventure, beauty, and sass.

Punjab, the land of the five rivers,
A state with a culture that never shivers.
From the fields of wheat to the Golden Temple,
It's a land of love, tradition, and sample.

Uttarakhand, the land of gods,
A state with a spirituality that's never at odds.
From the Char Dham Yatra to the Nanda Devi Peak,

It's a land of devotion, nature, and seek.

Uttar Pradesh, the heart of India,
A state with a history that's hard to define ya.
From the Taj Mahal to the Kashi Vishwanath Temple,
It's a land of culture, tradition, and ample.

Madhya Pradesh, the heart of India's culture,
A state with a heritage that's hard to nurture.
From the Khajuraho Temples to the Sanchi Stupa,
It's a land of art, history, and kuppa.

Gujarat, the land of the Mahatma,
A state with a culture that's hard to fathom.
From the Sabarmati Ashram to the Rann of Kutch,
It's a land of peace, tradition, and touch.

Rajasthan, the land of the royals,
A state with a charm that never coils.
From the forts of Jaipur to the sand dunes of Jaisalmer,
It's a land of splendor, history, and plumer.

Maharashtra, the land of dreams,
A state with a spirit that never screams.
From the Gateway of India to the Ajanta Caves,
It's a land of art, culture, and waves.

Goa, the land of the sun, sea, and sand,
A state with a beauty that's hard to withstand.
From the beaches of Baga to the churches of Old Goa,
It's a land of fun, relaxation, and glow.

Karnataka, the land of the Kannadigas,
A state with a language that never triggers.
From the ruins of Hampi to the Silicon Valley of India,
It's a land of technology, culture, and anuvida.

Kerala, the land of the gods,
A state with a charm that's hard to plod.
From the backwaters of Alleppey to the hill station of Munnar,
It's a land of beauty, serenity, and gala.

Tamil Nadu, the land of the Tamils,
A state with a language that's hard to dim.
From the temples of Madurai to the beaches of Chennai,
It's a land of culture, tradition, and runny.

Andhra Pradesh, the land of the Telugus,
A state with a heritage that's hard to refuse.
From the Charminar of Hyderabad to the beaches of Vizag,
It's a land of history, culture, and rag.

Telangana, the land of the Nizams,
A state with a culture that's hard to slam.
From the Golconda Fort to the Ramoji Film City,
It's a land of glamour, tradition, and witty.

Odisha, the land of temples and tribes,
A state with a beauty that never hides.
From the Sun Temple of Konark to the Jagannath Temple of Puri,
It's a land of art, tradition, and fury.

West Bengal, the land of the Tagores,
A state with a culture that never bores.

From the Victoria Memorial to the Sunderbans,
It's a land of history, literature, and bans.

Assam, the land of the mighty Brahmaputra,
A state with a beauty that's hard to sutra.
From the Kaziranga National Park to the Kamakhya Temple,
It's a land of nature, culture, and sample.

Meghalaya, the abode of clouds,
A state with a charm that's never in crowds.
From the living root bridges of Cherrapunji to the Umiam Lake,
It's a land of nature, adventure, and take.

Manipur, the jewel of India's east,
A state with a culture that's hard to beast.
From the Loktak Lake to the Kangla Fort,
It's a land of art, tradition, and port.

Mizoram, the land of the Mizos,
A state with a beauty that never slows.
From the Durtlang Hills to the Vantawng Falls,
It's a land of nature, culture, and calls.

Nagaland, the land of the Naga tribes,
A state with a heritage that never jibes.
From the Kohima War Cemetery to the Dzukou Valley,
It's a land of history, culture, and tally.

Sikkim, the land of the Kangchenjunga,
A state with a charm that's hard to wrunga.
From the Tsomgo Lake to the Rumtek Monastery,
It's a land of nature, spirituality, and mastery.

Tripura, the land of the Tripuris,
A state with a culture that never seizes.
From the Neermahal Palace to the Ujjayanta Palace,
It's a land of history, art, and solace.

These are the states of India,
Each with a charm that's hard to peal.
From the mountains to the seas,
India is a land of beauty, culture, and appease.

9 789356 676183